MW00904055

A Birth Day For Hannah

Photos & Story by Linda Petrie Bunch

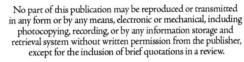

For Judy Petrie,
top dog saleswoman,
Thanks Mom!

Text & photographs copyright © 2017 Linda Petrie Bunch

No part of this publication may be reproduced or transmitted
in any form or by any means, electronic or mechanical, including
photocopying, recording, or by any information storage and
retrieval system without written permission from the publisher,
except for the inclusion of brief quotations in a review.

Printed in the United States of America
Book Club Productions

To order books visit MountainDogBooks.com
or write to hannah@mountaindogbooks.com.

Hannah is a woofer & a tweeter.
Follow her dog blog &
make friends with her on facebook!

Library of Congress Control Number: 2014912589
Petrie Bunch, Linda, author, photographer.
   A birth day for Hannah / photos & story by Linda
Petrie Bunch.
   pages cm
   SUMMARY: In this rhyming story, Hannah, a Bernese
mountain dog, gives birth to her first litter of puppies
and raises them until they are ready to go to their new
homes.
   Audience: Ages 0-10.
   ISBN-13: 978-0-9777781-2-6
   ISBN-10: 0-9777781-2-6

   1. Bernese mountain dog--Juvenile fiction.
2. Puppies--Juvenile fiction. 3. Stories in rhyme.
[1. Bernese mountain dog--Fiction. 2. Dogs--Fiction.
3. Birth--Fiction. 4. Stories in rhyme.]   I. Title.

   PZ8.3.P4575Bi 2017   [E]
                    QBI14-600120

Hannah the mountain dog
grew up very fast.
Being a puppy
was part of her past.

Hannah decided,
since she was full grown,
that she would have puppies
all of her own.

Then one special morning
Hannah gave birth
to nine little puppies,
their first day on earth!

Mom cleaned them all up
with kisses and licks,

and nursed with her milk between wiggles and kicks.

In two weeks they struggled
to open their eyes
to a colorful world
that was full of surprise.

Soon they were hearing
and starting to walk,
squeaking and squealing
and learning to talk.

They slept close together,
dogs piled in a mound,
a blanket of fur
around each little hound.

At four weeks the puppies
began to eat mush.
Slurping and burping,
they ate in a rush.

They grew strong and sturdy,
while sharing their toys.
Growling and barking,
they made lots of noise!

Hannah was clever,
smarter than smart,
but she couldn't tell
those doggies apart!

Their markings all matched.
They all looked the same.
So Hannah gave each pup
a wonderful name.

Katybeth, Oliver,
Lily, Kili and Dot,
Myers and Dougie,
and Ziggy and Spock...

all played well together
and slept quite a lot,
nosey and cozy,
and Dot had a spot!

The bouncing Bernese
formed a puppy parade,
prancing and dancing,
a marching brigade.

Pushing and pulling
they loved tug-of-war,
wrestling and wriggling
and howling for more!

Squirming and squiggling
and wiggling in tangles,
they twisted and twirled
into very strange angles.

Out in the garden
Dot stepped on the hose.
The mud puddle rose
up over their toes!

Pups rumbled and tumbled
in deep piles of dirt,
coats were all messy,
but no one got hurt.

Sad muddy puppies
were grubby and cold,
quivering and shivering,
too slippery to hold.

They jumped in the bathtub,
a warm bowl of bubbles,
to scrub up and clean up
without any troubles.

Nine fluffy puppies
all shiny and clean,
just like they'd been
in a washing machine!

It was time for a party
and a big birthday cake,
with candles and frosting...
better than steak!

Nine birthdays at once
was a huge celebration,
at eight weeks of age,
a tail-wagging occasion.

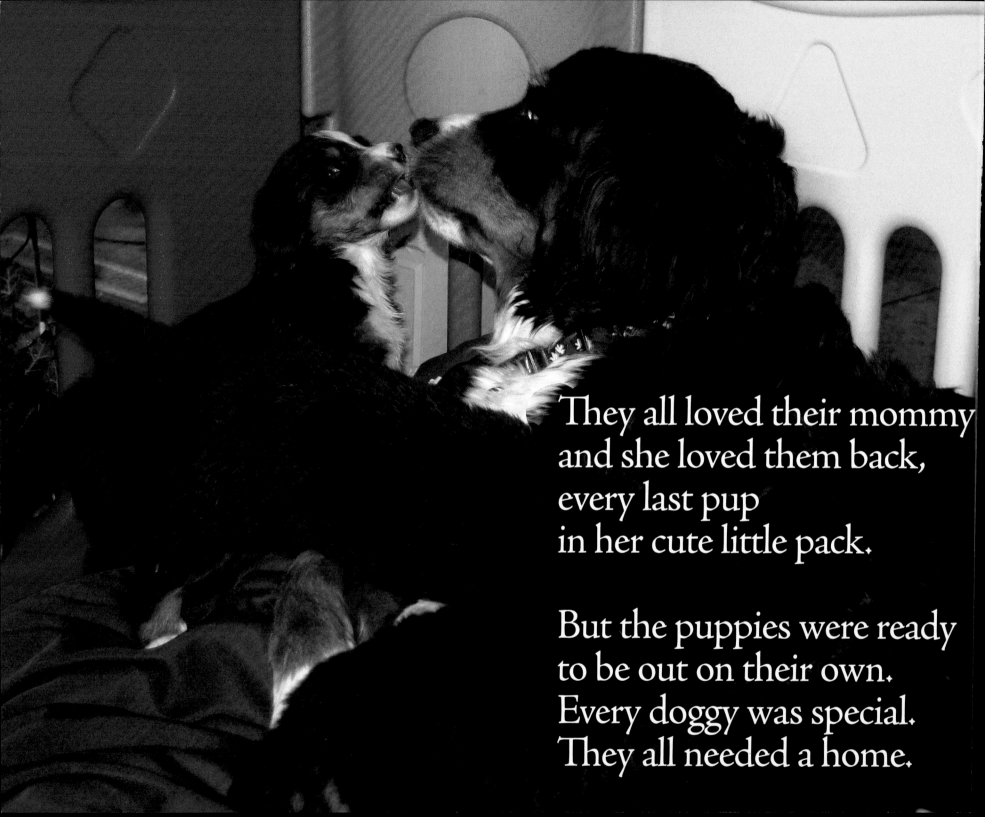

They all loved their mommy
and she loved them back,
every last pup
in her cute little pack.

But the puppies were ready
to be out on their own.
Every doggy was special.
They all needed a home.

Hannah sat and she watched.
Of course she felt sad.
Each dog found a family
and that made her glad.

And so one by one
they all went away...

But Hannah was lucky...
Dot got to stay!